Rainy Weather

For R.S.C.

First published in Great Britain by
HarperCollins Publishers Ltd in 1994
First published in Picture Lions in 1995
10 9 8 7 6 5 4 3 2 1
Picture Lions is an imprint of the Children's Division,
part of HarperCollins Publishers Ltd
Copyright © Mark Burgess 1994
A CIP catalogue record for this title
is available from the British Library.
The author asserts the moral right
to be identified as the author of the work.
ISBN: 0 00 664578 X
Printed and bound in Hong Kong

Rainy Weather

MARK BURGESS

PictureLions

An Imprint of HarperCollins*Publishers*

INTRODUCTION

A few years ago Hannah Hedgehog took over the little hotel by the sea from her Aunt Hetty. Hannah's aunt was tired of hotel life and had decided to travel the world in her hot air balloon.

These days Hannah's Hotel is the ideal place for a holiday. Hannah is helped by Molly Mouse; Sam Squirrel is the cook and Rodney Rabbit does all the odd jobs.

Everything is done to make the visitors happy. However, sometimes this isn't easy – such as when it just wouldn't stop raining.

"Oh, if only the rain would stop!" said Hannah as she came in through the back door.

"It's good for the garden," said Rodney, cheerfully.

"Huh! Well it's NOT good for the hotel," said Hannah.

It had been raining for weeks and, except for Dora Dormouse, Hannah's Hotel was empty. Nobody wanted to come to the hotel in so much rain.

"I wish someone would come and stay,"
said Hannah with a sigh.
"What anyone?
Even the gerbils?"
said Molly.
The last time
the gerbils had been they had had
an ice cream fight in the sitting room.
"Well..." said Hannah.
"I'd need my saucepans back first," said Sam.
"The skylight is still letting in the rain."
Sam's saucepans were scattered about
the landing to catch the drips.
"I'm going to mend it now," said Rodney.
"Good," said Hannah.
"Then at least we'll
be dry inside. But
don't you want a coat, Rodney?"
"No," said Rodney. "A little bit of rain
won't do me any harm."

Rodney had almost finished work
on the skylight when he heard
Hannah calling him.
"What is it?" said Rodney,
the rain dripping down
the back of his neck.

"Visitors," called Hannah.
"Can you go and
fetch them?"

"What?" said Rodney.

He couldn't hear because of the wind and rain. He climbed down the ladder.

"A Mr and Mrs Vole," said Hannah.
"They telephoned to say
their car has
broken down
and they want
to stay the night."
"All right, I'll go and fetch them,"
said Rodney. "I'll take the car as the tide's out.
Oh, and tell Sam he can have his saucepans
back – the skylight's fixed."
"Good," said Hannah.

The car wouldn't start.

Rodney opened the boot
to get out the tool box
and found Dora Dormouse
asleep inside.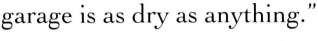

"Won't it go?" asked Dora, sleepily. "It's
probably damp. The Tootle 1.8 GTX suffers
with damp. It's a well known problem."
"It can't be damp," said Rodney. "The
garage is as dry as anything."

"Yes, but I spilt my tea over the engine,"
said Dora. "Don't worry, we'll get it started
in no time."

When Rodney reached the voles they were
having an argument.

"You had to take that short cut, didn't you?"
said Mrs Vole to her husband.

"We were late. We were going to miss our
plane," said Mr Vole.

"Well, we have missed it, haven't we? A nice
holiday in the sun, you said. And look at this
rain."

"Err... Hello," said Rodney.
"Why didn't you stop?" said Mrs Vole.
"What?" said Rodney.
"Not you," said Mrs Vole, getting into the car.

"I did stop," said Mr Vole.
"The water stopped the car, you mean," said Mrs Vole. "Fancy driving on when you saw the road was flooded!"

When they arrived at the hotel, Hannah and Molly were at the front door to meet them.

"Welcome to Hannah's Hotel," began Hannah.
"Everything will be –"
"I say you should have stopped sooner,"
said Mrs Vole.

"It's all your fault," said Mr Vole. "If you hadn't told me to turn right when it should've been left –"
"You said you had the whole route worked out!" shouted Mrs Vole.
"Let me show you to your rooms," said Hannah, loudly.
"Rodney will bring up your suitcases, won't you Rodney?"
Rodney nodded and then sneezed.

At last Hannah and Molly got the voles up to their room.
"I'll bring you some tea and scones," said Hannah as she closed the door on them.
They were still arguing.
"Ping" went the bell at reception.
"Who can that be?" said Molly.

It was Freddie Frog. He was wearing a pink swimsuit and was standing in a large pool of water.

"Lovely weather," he said.

"Err... yes," said Hannah, politely. She tried not to look at the wet carpet. "Would you like a room, Mr Frog?"

"Oh yes, please," said Freddie. "With a bath if you've got one."

"Yes, of course," said Hannah.

"How did you arrive, Mr Frog? We didn't see your car," said Molly.

"I swam," said Freddie. "I'm on a swimming tour, you see. All round the coast." He showed them a very damp map.
"How interesting," said Hannah.
"Now then, Mr Frog, Molly will show you to your room. Please make yourself at home."
"Oh, thank you. I shall," said Freddie.

Hannah went into the kitchen. Rodney was sitting huddled by the stove.
"Rodney's caught a chill," said Sam, who was making him some of his special elderflower cordial. Rodney sneezed.
"I think you should be in bed," said Hannah.
"Oh, I'll be all right," said Rodney, sniffing.

Freddie Frog decided to have a bath. He put
in the plug and turned the taps on full.
"Lovely!" he said
as the water came
gushing out.
"Now then, what
shall I wear this evening?
I must look smart."
Freddie went back into his bedroom and
tried on his stripy shirt with his blue trousers.

"That's it," he said,
looking in the mirror.
"Now, which bow tie?"
Freddie couldn't
make up his mind.
He'd have to
ask someone.
He opened the door
to his room and looked out.

Molly was going by
with a tray of tea things.
"Excuse me," said Freddie,
waving a bow tie.

"What is it, Mr Frog?"
said Molly.

"It's a bow tie," said Freddie.
"Here's another. Which do you like best?"
"Oh the red one, definitely," said Molly.
"Right, I'll wear that one," said Freddie.
As he turned back into
his room he caught sight
of his alarm clock. It was
almost eight o'clock.
Freddie finished
dressing and then
hurried downstairs
so as not to be late for dinner.

Sam was getting flustered.
He was behind with his cooking
and to make matters worse,
things kept going wrong.

First the soup boiled over.
Then he muddled tablespoons with teaspoons
and put too much salt in the spinach risotto.

He forgot to unwrap the cheese before
grating it so that the cauliflower sauce went
all lumpy.

And then in came Molly and took away
most of his saucepans.
"The skylight's leaking again," she said.
"Oh, BOTHER!" cried Sam, and he threw
the spaghetti at the wall.

The voles had stopped arguing by dinner time.
They ate without talking at all.
Freddie saw that
they looked
rather miserable
and tried to cheer them up.
"Lovely weather!" he said,
but then Mrs Vole burst into tears.

"I really don't think I can
eat any more soup,"
said Dora Dormouse,
who was sitting at
the next table.
"It's delicious but
I just don't seem to
be able to finish it."
"Don't worry," said
Hannah. "That's
odd, it looks
rather watery..."
"Mmm, lovely," said Freddie, tasting it.
Suddenly something splashed into the soup.
Everybody looked up.
Water was seeping through the ceiling.
"Oh, that leaky skylight..." said Hannah.
"That's not the skylight," said Molly. "That's
Room 6, Mr Frog's –"

"Ahh..." gasped Freddie, remembering his bath. "Ohh... Sorry!" and he dashed out of the dining room and up the stairs.

Freddie's room was awash. Hannah quickly pulled the plug out of the bath and turned off the taps.

"Sorry...Sorry..." said Freddie, paddling about.

"Well, this is a fine mess," said Hannah,

trying to remain calm. "It will take some
mopping up. We'll move you to another
room, Mr Frog. You won't want to
sleep here."
"Oh no, this is *quite* all right," said Freddie.
"Honestly."

The next morning it was still raining.
Hannah went to see how Rodney was.
"I dode feel doo good," said Rodney.
He stayed in bed.

Hannah was just finishing her breakfast
when the telephone
started ringing.
A flock of ducks
wanted to hold a
special meeting at
the hotel and would be
arriving that afternoon.
All twenty-five of them.

"It's going to be a busy day,"
said Hannah to Molly.
"We've got the ducks'
rooms to get ready
and, as Rodney's ill,
I'll have to drive
the voles to pick up
their car. The travel agent has
booked them on to another flight
so they'll get their holiday after all."

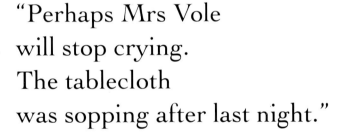

"They'll be pleased about that," said Molly.
"Perhaps Mrs Vole
will stop crying.
The tablecloth
was sopping after last night."

Freddie was looking at
the books in the lounge.
He found one called
The Great Lakes which he
thought looked interesting.
He was just about to
open it when he dropped
it behind a radiator.
He couldn't reach it.

Freddie looked about for something to push
the book out with.
He got a broom from
the broom cupboard
and poked it down
behind the radiator.
The broom got stuck.

"Ohh..." said Freddie,
tugging on the broom.

Freddie pulled
as hard as he could.
"That's it," he said as
the broom began to move. "One last tug..."
And then the radiator fell off the wall.
Water started pouring out of
the end of the pipe.

"Oh...Ohh..."
cried Freddie,
trying to stop it. But the water
just sprayed about like a fountain.

"What shall I do?"
he wailed. "What shall I do?"

Hannah was helping
the voles downstairs
with their cases.
"We're so grateful.
Aren't we, dear?" said Mr Vole.
"Yes," sobbed Mrs Vole. "I'm so happy."

"Hannah," said Sam,
coming out of the
kitchen. "How am I
supposed to cook for
twenty-five ducks with
three saucepans?"
"Don't worry Sam," said
Hannah. "The skylight will be
fixed. The builders will –"

Then her mouth dropped open as a book
floated out of the sitting room.

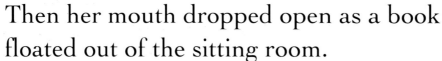

"It's all right," said Freddie, dashing out of
the office. "I've telephoned the builders.
They'll be here soon."
"Builders... Which builders?" said Hannah.
"Why, G&G Builders,"
said Freddie. "They said
they'd come straight away."

"But... that's the GERBILS!"
cried Hannah. "Oh NO!"

"Hannah," called Molly from upstairs.
"The ducks have arrived. There are twenty-four
splashing about in the swimming pool... And
now they're coming inside..."

Here are some more Picture Lions

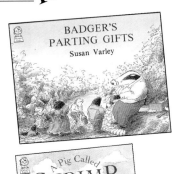

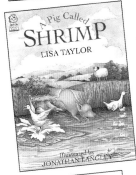

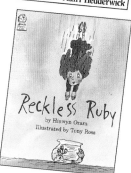

for you to enjoy